COMPANY MORALE

A BIMBO TRANSFORMATION NOVELLA

SADIE THATCHER

"Baby, don't go," Gisele pleaded with her boyfriend. "If you stay, I'll… I'll suck your cock."

Gisele was not normally so forward with Javier. She was not normally so forward at all. She was a hard working professional woman with serious career aspirations.

But it was Saturday and Javier had brought a prototype he had been developing at work. He could have gotten in big trouble for letting the device leave the lab, let alone taking it out himself, but the chance to have some fun with his girlfriend was too great a draw.

Gisele giggled at her own boldness. She never sucked Javier's cock. At least, she never did unless she was under the influence of the prototype. But given the circumstances, she would do anything to keep her boyfriend from leaving her that night.

"I told you," Javier explained. "I agreed to take my mother to church tomorrow. It's important."

Gisele was in no mood for seriousness. She wanted to play. That was almost entirely related to the prototype. It was essentially a brainwashing machine. It could give the user new ideas and change their mood. The changes were not extreme. It was more like a mood enhancement.

After a long week at work, Gisele had nearly canceled her weekend with Javier. That was until he offered to use the device on her. He had shared all the details before, keeping her completely informed about his work. He had not needed to. He wanted to. It was a sign of faith and trust in their relationship.

When Javier came over Friday night with the prototype, she had been hesitant to use it.

"Are you sure it's safe?" Gisele had asked.

"Absolutely," Javier said. "We've done extensive testing. I've even used it on myself. And I promise to use the device tomorrow so you can be ready for work on Monday. The whole thing is reversible."

Gisele was still hesitant as Javier started to wire her up, placing the electrodes on her temples, but she knew she needed a break. It had been a stressful week and spending 24 hours or so with her worries lifted from her shoulders sounded like just the vacation she needed.

And it had been. The "bimbo" setting Javier had used left Gisele feeling happy and free, without a care in the world. And that was before they had sex that day. Without her own brain getting in the way, sex with Javier was a whole new experience and one that she loved. Her body's responses felt so much stronger without her brain getting in the way, filtering out the pleasure.

And so, at the end of the day, Gisele was not only begging Javier to stay, but to let her spend another day as a bimbo.

"Please," Gisele begged again. Javier was already hooking her up to the prototype as she pleaded with him.

"I told you, I can't. But I'll tell you what, I'll leave it here so we can play with it next weekend. Now that I have it out of the lab, it might be easier for it to stay missing for a while.

And I would rather not have it at my place, in case the company finds out. If they decide to search my apartment, I can't hide it."

Even in her slightly bimbofied state, Gisele had to agree with that. His apartment was tiny. There was no way he could hide it. I would be safer in her hands, even if she did not dare use it.

"Okay, I'm all set," Javier said as he held up the device that he had connected to her temples. "Are you ready to go back to normal?"

Gisele bit her lower lip, looking dejected. But she accepted his expertise. It was his machine, after all. She nodded her head.

"Here we go," Javier said as he activated the machine on. It was already set to changing her back.

Gisele's world disappeared. The machine placed her into a blank state as it did its work to her mind. Javier had seen all the test results. She would be put back to just how she was before, as if the previous 24 hours had never happened, although she would remember all of it.

"Hmm, that's strange," Javier said as the machine spit out an error. The machine started to reset, acting like the "bimbo" program was starting afresh. Multiple uses would increase the effects of the machine and make Gisele act like even more of a bimbo.

While he figured that would be fun to experiment with in the future, Javier was not about to play that card now. He did need to go. It was late and he needed to be up early in the morning.

It was a simple fix to override the error message and force the machine to return Gisele to normality. It just required manual intervention. It was something to look into when he returned to the lab on Monday. He had simulations he could run, so he would not need the actual device present.

"How do you feel?" Javier asked as Gisele woke up.

She looked up at him and smiled. "Wow, I feel completely back to normal."

"So you aren't offering to suck my cock to keep me here anymore?"

Gisele blushed as that memory surfaced. Had she really done that? She must have. And the strange thing was, she had never actually given a blowjob before, so it was doubly strange for her to make such an offer.

"No, I can't see myself doing that," Gisele said. "At least not until next weekend when you make me a bimbo again."

"So you do want to do it again?" Javier asked. "I wasn't sure you would. I mean, it's not really your kind of thing."

"It was fun," Gisele admitted. "I mean, no, I wouldn't want to go out like that. It's bad enough having big boobs and having everyone treat me like I'm dumb, but this weekend was fun and it was a huge stress reliever. So depending on how work goes this next week, I could see doing this again."

This time it was Javier's turn to smile. He liked what he heard. It of course helped that Javier had been careful in setting up the parameters for his girlfriend. He had worked hard not to be too dominating, letting her take the lead a little in directing how far she wanted to take their activities. And he had been firm in keeping her at home, not even letting her out of the house. The chance she would be seen and people would think less than kindly of her worried him too much to let her take such risks.

Still, it had been fun for him too. And the sex had been fantastic. It was the best they had ever had as a couple. Bimbo Gisele was a firecracker in bed. She just kept going and going. Her enthusiasm was unmatched.

"As I said, if you can keep the prototype here, that would be a big help," Javier said. "I'll talk to you tomorrow. I have to go now. I love you."

"I love you too," Gisele said before they kissed each other good night.

She followed him to the front door and watched him through the window as he practically skipped down the front walk toward his car parked on the street. She continued to watch until he had driven away and out of sight.

It was only then, that she went to bed, sleeping peacefully, unconcerned about the stress she had brought home Friday from work and unknowing what was about to come.

G isele slept in Sunday morning. Unlike Javier, she was not particularly religious. She had grown up Catholic, but fallen out of the faith over time. Actually, Javier was not particularly religious either, but he maintained certain activities with the church for the sake of his mother, who was deeply religious.

Either way, Gisele enjoyed her morning in bed. She laid about, read part of a book she had been meaning to get to, and generally reveled in the afterglow from her fun mental excursion that was her weekend.

Eventually, however, the demands fo the real world hit her. She needed to prep several documents for Monday. Working the corporate life, focusing on moving up the ladder, made life difficult sometimes.

Gisele saw her old friends from high school and college post their adventures on social media. She knew what they posted were only small snapshots of their lives, but it sometimes hurt to see pictures from their travels and other adventures. They looked happy.

It was not that Gisele was unhappy, but she had long ago

decided to take the disciplined approach to moving up in the world. Given who she was and what she looked like, she knew she would have to work twice as hard as most other people to get where she wanted to go in life.

And thus far, that approach was paying off. She could see the light at the end of the tunnel as she neared the upper echelons of her company. And once she made it there, she was certain new doors would open for her. She would finally be earning the pay and benefits she knew she deserved and performing work that really mattered. She just had to pay her dues first.

Unfortunately, even as the light at the end of the tunnel seemed closer than ever, the work was harder than ever. Gisele found herself working longer hours with no additional pay. Her benefits were poor. Sick leave was handed out with an eye dropper.

Gisele lost her Sunday afternoon with her head buried in paperwork. There was more to do than she had at first assumed. It seemed one of the people she supervised did not finish his work before handing off the documents. It was easy enough to complete the work herself, just time consuming. But she would be having a talk with him on Monday, to voice her displeasure.

Normally Gisele would have sent the paperwork back to be fixed, but there was a reason this particular batch had come home with her on Friday. It needed to be completed by Monday morning. That put the responsibility on her shoulders.

As the afternoon wore on, Gisele found herself begin to worry about Javier. He usually reached out to her after taking his mother to church. It was sometimes a phone call, but he at least always texted her, letting her know he was thinking about her and maybe mentioning something interesting that happened at church that day.

But with each passing hour, it was becoming increasingly clear that something was wrong. Her texts went unanswered. Her calls went unanswered.

And then the bad news came. Javier had died. He had been driving his mother home after church. There was an accident. The other driver had been drunk.

Gisele saw it in a news alert. No one at the hospital had thought to contact her. They probably did not even know about her.

The hospital. Gisele had to go to the hospital. Her hands were shaking as she got behind the wheel of her car, but she was able to drive. She made it there safely only to have the news confirmed by hospital staff. Javier had perished. So too had his mother.

The drunk driver, on the other hand, walked away without a scratch. He was already in custody and would be officially charged Monday morning. This was not even his first drunk driving offense. He would be going away for a long time.

That was the only bright spot of the whole situation. Gisele was demoralized and heartbroken. She honestly did not know how she was going to go into work on Monday.

It would have been natural to take some time off after she lost the man she loved. It would have been normal. However, what was not normal was her company's policy on bereavement leave. It only applied to immediate family members, which she had found out when her uncle passed away. Javier, as her boyfriend, did not qualify.

It was a heartless policy and Gisele already planned to change it when she advanced to the point where she could advocate for such change.

To make matters worse, had already used up her sick leave and she could not afford to lose pay from a day off. Her mortgage had just gone up this year, leaving little left for the rest of her life. Her savings were shrinking fast as she spent more than she made each month.

With the bad news conformed, Gisele returned home. She did not know what else she could do. The hospital did not need or want her there. She would just be in the way. They offered for her to speak with a grief counselor, but none were available until next week.

It was a perfect storm to disrupt Gisele's life. Back at home, she quietly cried as she sat on the couch hugging her knees. She did not know how she was going to go on. She was not even at the point where she could move on. She was in shock.

It was only after Gisele cried herself out when she was finally able to think. She needed to make a plan. That was what she was good at. She was a great planner. It was what made her a valuable employee, looking ahead to foresee the risks and rewards of every action.

Obviously, she had failed to properly plan for what happened to Javier, but she was determined to create a new path forward for herself.

"I need to go to work tomorrow," Gisele told herself. That was the first step. Given her current situation, she needed to continue working. She would take time off for the funeral, if needed, but she could not take more time than that, as hard as that was to admit. She wanted to honor Javier's memory, but she needed to do so while maintaining her work schedule.

"But how?" Gisele asked herself next. How could she go to work when her heart ached as it did? The pain and loss were so fresh. How could she be productive in her current state?

Gisele thought about her options. All of them were bad. She really felt like her only option was to not go into work on Monday. She would take the pay hit, as hard as that was to stomach, but she would have time to process her feelings.

She wished there was a way to alter her state, to take away her worries and her pain, at least until she could get through the workday.

The idea was heartless. It was soulless. It also seemed impossible. How could she set aside her pain like that, deny that which made her human?

And then the solution came to her. Her face brightened as she realized there was one thing that could make it all work out. Javier's prototype. That was the answer. She could use the device on herself, just for the day so she could get work done. The bimbo version of herself might be less productive than Gisele usually was, but she would be productive compared to her in her current state.

"Thank you, Javier," Gisele said as she sprang into action. She would deal with the pain another time. For now, she needed peace. The prototype could give her that peace.

That night, as Gisele tried to fall asleep, she realized waiting to use the machine was no longer an option. She could not sleep with her thoughts still focused on Javier. For her to have any hope of getting something close to a full night's sleep, she needed to go to use the device now and then let herself sleep in peace.

Wearing her nightgown, Gisele pulled out Javier's prototype. Just holding it again, knowing he had built it, made her heart ache. She quietly sobbed for several minutes, her eyes remaining dry. Her body was spent in that regards.

Finally, determination returned. Gisele pulled out the device from under the bed, the simplest of hiding places, and began to connect the contacts to her temples, just as Javier had done before.

He had shown her how to operate the machine. It was simple and the "bimbo" setting came pre-programmed. When she turned on the machine, that setting was already selected. Then all she had to do was activate the device.

As soon as Gisele pushed the button, her mind went blank and her vision turned black. She was unaware of anything and everything as the machine gave her a bimbo mindset.

When she awoke sometime later, Gisele felt like a whole new person. She was still aware of the news. She knew her boyfriend was gone. But the pain was gone. She could still sense it. She could still feel a deep sadness over Javier's passing, but she was detached from it. Her negative emotions were a separate entity that she could choose to deal with or not deal with at her leisure.

And with the immediate crisis at least dealt with, Gisele yawned before climbing back into bed for a good night's sleep.

MONDAY

When Gisele woke Monday morning, even the pulsing scream of her alarm could not wipe the smile off her face. She felt good, like she could grab the world by the tail and wrestle it to better fit her liking.

It was only once Gisele stepped into the shower that she remembered the events of the day before. Her smile faded, sadness gripped her heart. However, it was a manageable sadness. It was not overbearing and disabling as it had been before. She could handle it.

"Hi, Martha," Gisele said as she greeted her cubicle neighbor on her walk into work.

"You're here?" Martha said, shocked at Gisele's presence.

"Yes, I'm here," Gisele answered calmly. "I can't afford not to be."

Martha was aware of Gisele's money situation. They had several long talks about mortgages and home buying before Gisele pulled the trigger and bought her house. She knew how much Gisele had to work to keep herself current on the mortgage.

"But…" Martha started to say before she paused to make sure she got her wording right. "You heard about the news last night, right?"

"Yes, I'm aware," Gisele said in a detached way. "It's all very sad."

"That's it?" Martha asked in shock. "It's just sad."

"Look," Gisele said, trying to find the right words. Words were not exactly her strong suit when she was under the effects fo the prototype. "I am trying to stay put together for work right now. We both know the company wouldn't allow me to take the time off I need."

"Okay," Martha said. "You have my condolences. If there's anything you need, let me know."

"Will do," Gisele said. "Now I really must get to work."

Gisele managed to finish her paperwork and get it turned in before anyone came looking for it. After that, she spent the rest of her workday connecting with her team and responding to emails that had piled up over the weekend.

For the most part, no one noticed a significant change in Gisele's work behavior. Her more bimboish attitudes were counterbalanced by the pain she still felt. It gave her the same seriousness she always had, but in a more light hearted way. She did not share the news of the weekend with her team, but they appreciated her kinder nature as she spoke to them.

But keeping up the facade was difficult for Gisele. She found herself nearly hyperventilating in the bathroom three separate times. She knew she needed to feel all the different feelings the device was helping her keep at bay, but she also knew she needed to keep chugging along. She could not pause her life.

It was on Gisele's drive home from work that she began to ponder what she should do next. She had made it through the workday receiving high marks from both her superiors and her subordinates. But it all felt like a sham. Gisele put on a strong face, but she needed to deal with everything head on. She could not dodge her negative feelings forever. They were an important part of her and she could not ignore them forever. She needed to reverse the process and focus on her mental health properly.

However, once Gisele reached home, she found herself in no mood to turn off the bimbo. She could feel the weight of her grief in the background. Just the thought of once again carrying that on her shoulder gave her anxiety. She was not the happy bimbo she had been over the weekend. She was nervous and anxious and skittish.

But rather than use the machine to change herself back, Gisele tried to distract herself and stay busy. She made herself a nice dinner, breaking out the grill for the first time of the year. Then she found a movie she wanted to watch. It was a comedy that made her laugh.

It was only after all of that, once Gisele had her fill of mindless entertainment, that she began to realize she needed to turn off her bimbo mode. It was time to accept reality and start processing her emotions.

It was with great regret that Gisele hooked herself up to the device again. She feared the anxiety and sadness that she knew would envelope her. She did not want it to reach her, even if she had every intention of working through her pent up feelings eventually. She just did not want that time to be now.

Once everything was hooked up, Gisele activated the machine. It began to hum. Then her vision went dark and shew as lost to whatever the machine did to change her brain.

Gisele had no knowledge of the fault in the device. Javier had been able to fix it in real time, but she was now using the machine without supervision. And with her out of commission while the machine did its work, there was no one to watch over her and correct the error when it appeared.

Rather than undo the bimbo mode she had been placed in, the error reset the machine and forced her through another bimbofying loop. Gisele was completely unaware of this fact as it happened. Her mind had been silenced until the device had completed its work. She had no idea what it was doing to her.

When Gisele came to after the machine had finished its work and shut itself off, she looked around her bedroom with a degree of confusion.

"What just happened?" she asked out loud. She looked down to see the device in front of her and the memories from before she had used it started to return to her.

"Oh yeah," she said. "I was changing back."

Then Gisele did something she had never done before. She giggled. She barely registered she had done it. Yes, it was odd, but in the moment, she could not see odd as being bad. It was just odd.

Gisele took her time putting the device away, stashing it underneath her bed once again. It worked well for a hiding place. It certainly kept it out of her normal line of sight, preventing her from thinking about it too much. She did not want to tempt herself to use the device unless she really needed to.

Taking a deep breath, Gisele took her time before she began to try and think about the events of the weekend. However, there was something strange about it all. It felt as if the sadness and turmoil of Sunday's news was even farther away than before. She felt less concerned about it all than before.

"Maybe I'm okie dokie," Gisele pondered to herself. She certainly felt good. She barely registered the loss of the man she loved. She knew the facts, but the emotion was not there, drowned out by a positivity she could only describe as bimboish.

And if that fact should have concerned her, it did not. Gisele let out a contented sigh and went to bed. She would pick up where she left off later. For now, her bed was calling her to get her beauty sleep.

Gisele woke up Tuesday morning with a smile on her face. She sat up and quietly stretched as she enjoyed the warm rays of the sun peaking through the curtains.

She took her time getting going and starting her day. She felt happy and relaxed, like waking up on a warm sunny day in the summer, without having to worry about anything.

Of course, that was not entirely true. She did have things to worry about. Chiefly she needed to get ready for work. Still, Gisele found herself taking it slow and cherishing every moment. The events of Sunday seemed like a distant memory, one she had no interest in exploring.

When Gisele showed up at work, she was smiling. That smile did not even go away when Martha asked her what made her late.

"I felt too good this morning not to take my time," Gisele answered. "It's a beautiful morning."

"You're not on drugs, are you?" Martha asked. "Because seeing you smile after what happened… It's just weird."

Gisele did not know how to respond. Drugs? Of course

she was not on drugs. What kind of question was that? She was just feeling good.

Then it hit her. The device. Something had gone wrong. Instead of taking her out of bimbo mode, it added another layer. No wonder she was feeling so good. No wonder she had a hard time feeling sadness, or the multitude of other emotions she should have been feeling, over her boyfriend's untimely demise.

"Don't worry," Gisele said. "It's not drugs. I guess I just process loss differently than other people."

It was a lame excuse, but one Gisele knew Martha would be unable to refute. Still, it worried her that such a thing had happened. She had unknowingly subjected herself to another layer of bimbofication. If it were not for the fact she could not feel worry, she would have been deeply worried about that.

Then there was the matter of Gisele's choice of outfit. She looked professional. She always did. But this morning she had been a little more bold in her outfit selection, namely leaving an extra button undone to allow for her breasts to be seen. It was just a hint of cleavage, but it was more than she had ever shown off before.

It was impossible to hide the size of Gisele's breasts. They were simply too big. It was genetic. Every woman in her family was large in the chest. No one seemed to mind. If anything, the women in her family had never been left wanting for male attention. Gisele herself had to chase some men off with a stick to keep from hitting on her.

That was something she had liked about Javier. He saw her as more than just a set of boobs to look at and play with. And he was happy to take the lead and chase the staring creeps off. The fact they would do it even when she was completely covered and hanging on his arm was reason enough for him to take care of the problem.

Gisele had always been conservative in how she dressed. That was true at work as well as out in the wide world. She owned a total to two tops that naturally showed any cleavage. She exclusively wore them at home. Her boyfriend was the only one who ever saw her wearing them. Not even the delivery guy saw her wearing those tops. She would throw on a sweatshirt if someone came to the door.

But today was different. Gisele had not paid much attention as she got ready for work. She let her body operate on autopilot as she relaxed and reveled in the delicious feelings coursing through her body. It was only after arriving at work that she noticed her neckline was a little lower than usual.

Gisele could have closed up her top. The blouse had buttons. She could fix her fashion mistake, if it could really be called that, but she found her hands unwilling to respond to the idea. And so she went about her day showing more cleavage than she had ever imagined before.

The odd thing about that was Gisele did not feel embarrassed about her slightly more suggestive outfit. Normally her cheeks would have been burning red in her situation, but she felt just fine. She felt good even.

There were definitely a few men who found their eyes drawn to her chest more. She found more people looking at and talking to her breasts than before, but that too was not a bad feeling. She felt a strange sort of pride in being one of those women who men might drool over. She certainly did not see herself as drool worthy, at least not yet, but she could see how she might like it.

Unfortunately, Gisele's work was a bit more affected by her mental state. The balance she had struck Monday had been tipped in favor of the bimbo side of her. She still did her work, but she found her management style shifting. Her hard edge was disappearing. It seemed more important to keep the employees she supervised happy rather than keep the work on track.

Luckily, a one-day dip in productivity would not show up on any efficiency reports. If it did, it would be hidden under a mountain of data with no clear understanding that Gisele had not been her normal self on a Tuesday. And that was assuming there would be an overall drop at all. Gisele figured it would all average out in the end.

"Is there anything I can do for you to help you deal with, you know?" Martha asked at the end of the day.

Gisele had run out of activities to keep herself occupied with about 30 minutes left in the workday. There was still work to be done, but she did not have the mentally energy to continue to tackle them. Instead, she had turned to surfing the interest looking at clothes and reading up on workplace fashion. If Martha noticed Gisele was not working, she did not show it.

"Thanks for asking," Gisele said, completely aware that she should be grieving, even though she did not feel like it. Grief was such a negative emotion. She understood she needed to experience it at some point, but she much preferred feeling happy. "But I'm okay right now. I'll let you know if there's anything you can do."

It was on Gisele's drive home from work when she began to understand why her grieving process might be different from other people's in her instance. There was no one to grieve with. She shared no friends with Javier. They came from similar worlds, but there was no overlap. Not even Martha had met him and Martha was the closest person she had to a friend.

Family was not much help either. Javier just had his mother. There was no one in his family she could commiserate with. She was on her own.

However, even that realization did not make the events of

Sunday feel anymore real. It felt like a distant memory, a bad dream that left her feeling strange, but not bad.

"I have to reverse this bimbo thing," Gisele told herself as soon as she stepped into her house.

She had meant to go straight to her bedroom to use the device, but her trip through the kitchen reminded her she needed to eat first. Then, once she was eating, she felt the need for some entertainment. The television was such an easy way to divert herself for an hour or two.

And as it turned out, reality programming was a great way to have fun and pass the time. Gisele had never considered it enjoyable before, but now, it was different. She smiled and laughed, enjoying the instigated drama in other people's lives.

It was only when Gisele began to grow sleepy that night that she remembered her plan to reverse the bimbo effects fo the device. She turned off the television and finally made it to her bedroom, pulling the machine out from under the bed.

It took Gisele an extra moment than before to make sure she hooked herself up to the device correctly. There were wires and switches that seemed far more complicated than they had previously. But she did it. And when she turned on the machine, her world went blank and the machine did its work.

The error message returned, and just like Monday night, that errors set the machine to add another layer of bimbo programming to Gisele's mind rather than remove the previous layer. She was getting deeper.

When the machine finished, shutting itself off, Gisele woke up, but did not bother to put the machine away. She was tired and wanted to sleep. Since she wanted to sleep, that was exactly what she did. She climbed under the covers and was asleep within seconds of her head hitting the pillow.

WEDNESDAY

"Good morning, world," Gisele said as she sat up in bed and stretched. She looked around to see her bedroom filled with light. It made her feel light and happy, both feelings she found most enjoyable.

Her eyes ignored the device resting on her nightstand. She was uninterested in that at the moment. She was much more interested in getting dressed. It was a beautiful day and she wanted to take full advantage.

Gisele's shower took a little longer than usual. As she soaped up her body, her arousal spiked. When she began to wash her breasts, it spiked again.

"Oof," Gisele said as she felt her arousal rise to levels that could not be ignored. She was not a naturally horny woman. She had her moments, but those were few and far between. She was rarely someone who needed to masturbate.

However, this morning she did. As the hot spray continued to splatter against her skin, Gisele reached down between her legs. Her pussy was ready and waiting as two fingers slipped inside. Her thumb pushed against her clit, sending waves of pleasure up into Gisele's head.

Moments later, a third finger joined the other two, driving her arousal and pleasure even higher. Gisele was in heaven at her own ministrations. She felt absolutely delicious as she worked her way up toward the summit of her climax. She could feel the energy building high and higher within her, waiting for the dam to finally break and release all that built up pressure.

When Gisele finally came, her knees buckled and she dropped to the floor, thankfully without hurting herself. Her eyes rolled up into her head as the pleasure overwhelmed her. The release was immediate, but it felt like it took forever for her body to process all of the endorphins and other hormones that would leave her sated, but hopeful for more.

Suffice it to say, Gisele was even later getting into work that morning. Her self-play in the shower had taken far more time than she had bargained for. Not that she was worried or complaining. Both of those things would have clashed with her happy and light hearted attitude, which she now had in spades.

"I had to cover for you this morning," Martha hissed when Gisele finally made it to her cubicle. "I didn't know what to say, but you're supposed to call Mr. Marshall as soon as you can."

"Thanks, Martha," Gisele said. "You're a real doll. I'll get right on that."

Gisele had never sued such language around Martha before. She had always been the consummate professional. Calling someone a doll did not exactly live up to those standards. Had Gisele been a man, she likely would have been reprimanded for sexual harassment. As it was, Martha was too surprised by her coworker's behavior to say anything.

As soon as Gisele dropped her purse in her file cabinet, she picked up the phone and dialed Mr. Marshall, her supervisor.

"Hi, Mr. Marshall," Gisele said. "This is Gisele. Martha said you wanted to talk to me."

"Ms. Torres," Mr Marshall began to speak. He sounded angry. His voice was loud enough Gisele had to hold the phone a little ways from her ear. "You were late this morning. What do you have to say for yourself?"

"I'm sorry, sir," Gisele responded. "There was a family matter. There was a death. I'm trying my best, sir."

Mr. Marshall's voice softened. "I'm sorry to hear about that. You are, however, aware of our bereavement leave policy, correct?"

"Yes, sir," Gisele answered. "I'm not asking for time off. I will do my best not to be late again."

"Good," Mr. Marshall said. "See that it doesn't. Otherwise, you can expect to see your role here to be changing. We expect all employees to give everything they can. It's why we're one of the best."

"Thank you, sir," Gisele said. She had stopped listening as soon as he went into his spiel about how great the company was. He was an example of the poor and shortsighted leadership at the company. She knew if she got promoted into a position of power, she would make the employees happier so they would do better work and have more loyalty.

Mr. Marshall hung up, leaving Gisele sitting there for several moments listening to a dial tone.

"Oopsie," Gisele said when she realized she had been twirling her hair without anyone on the line. "Well, back to work."

However, work did not go as well as she had hoped. Gisele felt overwhelmed by the status updates she received from the people she oversaw. Then there was the matter of the monthly spreadsheet. It tracked outside expenses, as well as certain performance metrics. She had been completing one each and every month since she was last promoted. It was the sort of thing she could do in her sleep.

But this time, Gisele would just stare at the spreadsheet, not really understanding what she was looking at. It all of a sudden seemed too complicated for her. She was afraid to touch it, fearful she might break it if she did.

After a sitting there for a while, a familiar feeling from her morning began to invade her thoughts. Her arousal had returned and it was building fast enough where she could not wait until after work for relief. She needed to take a break as soon as possible to relieve herself.

Gisele bit her lip as she came in the lady's washroom. She sat on the toilet, her skirt around her knees, and a hand buried in her pussy. The sense of relief was exquisite. Her body convulsed slightly as she came, but she made sure not to make a sound. There was no one else in the restroom at the time, but that could change at a moment's notice. And Gisele had no idea how thick the walls were. She did not want to draw unwanted attention to herself.

As it turned out, Gisele needed two more similar breaks throughout the day. By her mid-afternoon break, she was actually looking forward to the distraction. Work was suddenly boring for her. Other than her need for a paycheck, she honestly wondered why she bothered to keep showing up. Work was becoming a drag.

As soon as Gisele was done for the day, she was out of the office like a rocket. As she drove home, her right hand kept drifting underneath her skirt at stoplights. Her pussy was demanding attention again.

Gisele had never cum so many times in a single day before. Not even when she went bimbo for Javier over the weekend had she cum this much, and that had been a pretty sex-filled day. It felt like once she had activated the piping with her morning ministrations, she had been unable to turn it off. The tap was running and the bucket that was her arousal kept filling back up after she dumped the bucket with each orgasm. It was non-stop.

Fingering herself in the car had only served to raise her arousal and need to cum. She rushed into the house as soon as she was home and made a bee-line for her bedroom. Before she even thought about what she as doing, she had shucked off her work clothes and was lying back on the bed with one hand between her legs and the other massaging her breasts.

She came three times before she finally felt sated. Part of that was the distraction of hunger seemed to stem the flow of arousal. She needed to eat. And then she needed to use that infernal machine and turn off her bimbo mode. It was getting ridiculous that she was still playing bimbo this far into the week.

It was no longer about her sadness over Javier's death. Now it was about how her body kept demanding more attention than she could give it.

Not that Gisele remembered to use the device until she returned to her bedroom to go to sleep. After a satisfying dinner, she spent the rest of her evening watching trashy television while she gently rubbed at her clit. She did not even realize she was doing the latter. After her earlier ministrations in the nude, she had only put on a robe to make dinner. That meant she had easy access hours later as she mindlessly masturbated in front of the television.

"Oh yeah," Gisele said when she saw the device on her nightstand. "I need to use that."

It took longer than ever to attached herself to the machine, but once she turned it on and activated it, it went straight to work. And just like before, the error hit and the machine reverted to adding another layer of bimbo mode to Gisele's brain.

And like the night before, Gisele did not bother to put the machine away. Instead, she shirked off her robe and climbed under the covers to fall asleep.

G isele woke up Thursday morning with her fingers already in her pussy, mildly masturbating to whatever dream she had been having. The dream went unremembered, but that did not stop Gisele from continuing her ministrations.

Gisele collapsed back into bed following her orgasm. She laid there for several minutes, reveling in the pleasure that now always seemed to be present in her body. She felt amazing, signified by the big smile on her face.

When Gisele rolled into work, she was late again, even more so than before. She did not see her tardiness as her fault. After all, she needed to cum again in the shower. And then there was the trouble of finding an outfit she wanted to wear to work.

Everything in Gisele's closet seemed so drab and boring now. She had no interest in any of it. She had half a mind to wear one of her really low-cut tops with a short skirt. But deep down, she knew that was not professional enough.

Still, Gisele had prided herself in the end result of her outfit. Her high heels were the tallest thing she had to wear, lifting her ass and forcing her to stick out her chest. Her ass was well displayed wearing the tightest and shortest professional skirt she owned. It looked good, especially with the black stockings she wore with the seam straight up the back.

Gisele's blouse now definitely showed off her cleavage. She could no longer imagine dressing without showing off her breasts. They were her best feature and she wanted everyone to know that now. Not that much of her blouse was visible. Gisele's jacket covered most of it. And it was tight enough to further enhance her cleavage, lifting her breasts and pushing them together.

The men in the office were certainly noticing Gisele's change in style. Martha did too, although simply from an observational standpoint.

"You're really changing things up this week," Martha commented when Gisele finally showed up to work. "I mean, you look great, don't get me wrong, but I've never seen you dress like this before. Are you sure you don't want to talk about Javier?"

"Who?" Gisele asked, forgetting the tragic events of the past weekend for a moment. "Oh, Javier. No, I'm doing just fine. He left me something that has really been helping me deal with things."

Martha wanted to pry. She had so many questions. But she had the taste and wherewithal not to dig too deep unless Gisele was forthcoming with answered. At the moment, she was not and so Martha relented to leave things as they were.

Even though Martha and Gisele were not close friends, they had developed a friendliness since becoming cubicle neighbors. They looked out for each other. Martha only wanted what was best for Gisele. She would make herself available, but she knew she could not force Gisele to talk about her feelings.

Gisele did not remain in her cubicle for long. While she

seemed to have escaped the ire of upper management, she still had work to perform. Rather than check in on her team remotely as she usually did, Gisele took it upon herself to check in with them in person. She wanted to be more than just a screen name on a chat program or a face on a video call. And considering most of the people on her team were in the building, she decided to take a walk and visit with all of them personally.

The morning went swimmingly for Gisele. Each person she checked in with appreciated the time she took to visit them. She got to know everyone on her team better and they got to see she was not just some mindless middle manager. What was more, Gisele got to show off. The men focused on her breasts. That was fine by her. The women seemed to respond better to her smile. Whatever it took to motivate her team was fine by her.

However, after a morning spent wandering the office and talking to people, Gisele needed a break. She arousal was building again. She held her legs together when she stood still for any length of time, trying to take her mind off the pressure building between her legs.

From an outside observer, it looked like Gisele needed to pee. She, however, knew otherwise. She was horny and she needed to cum.

As Gisele made her way to the washroom, she found herself following behind Peter Marshall, the son of her boss, Mr. Marshall. Peter was a new hire at the company, fresh out of college and starting in the copy room. No one expected for him to be there for long. If history was any indication, he would have a management position, like his father, within three years. The other managers needed someplace to put him while they evaluated his skillset. That meant, he spent his time in the interim making copies and delivering printed materials around the office.

Peter must have heard Gisele following him as he turned. "It's Ms. Torres, right?" he asked. "I'm Peter Marshall."

"Please, you can call me Gisele," she responded as she shook his hand. She noted that while his eyes started out looking her in the face, his gaze had shifted downward. That only served to brighten Gisele's smile.

"It's nice to meet you finally," Peter said. "You can call me Peter if you'd like."

The details of what happened next were not exactly clear. Neither Peter nor Gisele could seem to remember them accurately. All that matters is that within minutes of their chance meeting, Gisele was on her knees in the copy room giving Peter the best blowjob of his life.

The even stranger part was Gisele had never sucked a cock in her life. But as soon as she found herself on her knees with Peter's cock in her face, she turned off her brain and simply operated on instinct.

"That's amazing," Peter said as he gently guided Gisele by the head as she slowly fucked her face. It was a combined effort, Peter guiding her and Gisele doing her best to pleasure the son of her boss.

When Peter came, he came hard, shooting rope after rope of hot white cum into Gisele's waiting mouth. She kept up her sucking efforts, letting her mouth fill with his seed, but it was too much. Rivulets of cum formed at the sides of her mouth, dripping down her chin.

Gisele was surprised too. Not only was she blowing a colleague, especially one who was definitely her inferior for the time being, but she was actually enjoying it. She more than enjoyed it. She loved it.

"Wow," Peter said as he watched Gisele slowly swallow his cum before trying to lick up what she had spilled. She ended up using her fingers to push what had dribbled onto her chin into her mouth.

"Yum," she found herself saying. It was her first time tasting cum and she had already realized it would not be her last. How could she not do that again? She had always thought blowjobs were degrading and gross. But she found her first attempt to be hot and fun. And there was a certain kind of pleasure to be derived from pleasing someone else.

"I don't mean to pry, but since I'm new, I just want to be sure," Peter began to say. "Are you the office slut or something?"

In the past, Gisele would have been angry at that question. Her a slut? Her the office slut? No. That was impossible. But now? Maybe not the office slut, but if blowing a guy she just met at work made her a slut, then she was going to have to live with that label. Maybe she was a slut, at least a little bit.

"Um, no," Gisele said as she pushed herself to her feet. She took a moment to make sure her outfit was not too rumpled and that her seams were straight. "I just... Well... I don't know. It just seemed like the right thing to do in the moment."

"I can't argue with that," Peter agreed. "If you ever want a repeat, you know where to find me."

"Thanks," Gisele said as she moved toward the door. She paused and looked back at the young man, licking her lips. She was not that much older than him, but he still had a lot of maturing to do in the next couple of years. "I'm sure I'll see you around."

And with that Gisele made her walk of shame back to her cubicle. She completely forgot about going to the washroom to get herself off. After blowing Peter, it did not seem as important anymore. Anyway, it was lunchtime and she was getting hungry. Her serving of cum did little to satisfy her appetite.

The rest of the afternoon went much as Wednesday had.

Gisele eventually found herself in the washroom for relief breaks. That was how she phrased them in her mind so that she had a valid excuse for not being at her desk should Mr. Marshall or someone else need her. Luckily, no one did.

However, unlike her previous trips home at the end of the workday, Gisele did not find herself going straight home. Instead, she found herself pulling into the parking lot at the mall.

By this point, Gisele had given up trying to analyze her actions. After sucking Peter's cock, going shopping seemed trivial. But the truth was, Gisele knew her wardrobe would need a significant upgrade. She was wearing her best work outfit and she could not continue to wear it day after day. She needed to change things up, while still maintaining a certain amount of professionalism.

And then there was her casual wardrobe. Gisele could barely look at most of those clothes, let alone wear them. She had no idea what she as thinking. Nor did she want to try and think about what she was previously thinking. It was much better to just dive in and act rather than think about it. And that was why she was shopping. She was taking action. She was going to enjoy it too.

Gisele spent all evening at the mall, going from store to store, buying anything and everything that caught her eye. Her new work clothes would push the boundaries of office appropriateness, but she was pretty sure she could stop herself from crossing over into pink slip territory.

Then there was the matter of casual clothes. Before, Giselle mostly lived in baggy jeans and loose sweatshirts. Given her new dispositions, however, none of those items would work. Even clothing meant for casual moments needed to place her body on display. What was the point of having big boobs if not to show them off? That was Gisele's reasoning, at least.

And show them off she would. Gisele found plenty of fun tops to wear, many that would not be appropriate to wear a bra with. But even her bras needed replacing. The old Gisele had been about minimizing her chest and hiding it away. The bimbo version fo Gisele wanted the opposite. She wanted the world to know she had big boobs and that she liked to show them off and have people look. There was a sexiness to boobs that Gisele had never contemplated before.

Not that she was contemplating much now. Instead, she simply knew big boobs and sexiness went hand-in-hand. It was part of the bimbo creed that she now followed. Sexy was good. Covering up was boring and bad.

When Gisele arrived home late the night, she wore a white halter top with a deep neckline that barely restrained her tits. It contrasted nicely against her dark skin. The pink circle skirt she wore might have been more feminine than even the bimbo Gisele would normally choose, but she liked how it swished around her thighs when she moved. And there was a guy at the mall who kept staring at her ass when she was trying it on, sealing the deal.

It took Gisele an hour to put away her new purchases. She had to completely purge her closet before she found room for everything. She was not sure if she would be donating the three large trash bags that were her previous clothes or if she would just throw them away. As much as she knew donating them was the right thing to do so that they might find a new life, but there was a part of her that never wanted anyone to be tempted to wear such dreadful clothes. It might be better to take them completely out of circulation to save other women from her previous fate.

It was only after she had put away all her new purchases that Gisele found herself getting ready for bed. That had become easy. She stripped out of her clothes and climbed under the covers. This time, however, without even thinking about it, Gisele pulled the device off the nightstand and began to hook herself up to it. She operated on pure muscle memory as she turned it on and went blissfully blank and another layer of bimbo mode was added to her already bimbofied mind.

When she was done, Gisele returned the machine to the nightstand and fell asleep to blissful dreams full of fun and sex.

FRIDAY

G isele woke up with an orgasm. Her fingers had found their way to her pussy in the night, as they seemed to naturally now. But it was her orgasm that woke her.

She laid back and reveled in the afterglow of her latest climax. She felt good. She felt really good. It was only when her alarm went off that she remembered that she needed to go to work. It was Friday, after all. It was the last day of the workweek.

"I wish it was casual Friday," Gisele said as she perused her closet for her next outfit. The purchases she had made the night before had been good, but she wanted to wear something fun and sexy to the office, not something drab and "professional." Gisele was not even sure what that meant anymore. As long ass work could get done while wearing it, she figured that should count for professional. Unfortunately, that was not up to her.

Despite getting out of bed with her alarm, Gisele was still late for work. It had taken her three times to get her makeup right. The trouble had been her eyeshadow. First she had not put on enough. Then she had put on too much—and there was such a thing as too much—before she finally got it right.

The trouble came from the fact each time she redid her eyeshadow, she felt the need to start over from the beginning, meaning it required three attempts at putting on all of her makeup, twice washing her face clean to start again.

"Um," Martha said when Gisele sashayed by her cubicle. "You're nearly two hours late and you look like you're leaving work for a date, not arriving."

Martha hated to be so judgmental, but she figured enough was enough with Gisele's strange behavior. She was certain this was not emotionally productive.

"Oh," Gisele said, not knowing what else to say. She looked confused. "I wanted to look nice today. It's Friday."

Martha gaped at her coworker. As if it being Friday explained anything. It was just a day of the week. It was not special. Yes, it was the last day of the workweek, but that was no excuse. It was not reason to celebrate. As far as Martha was concerned, celebrations could begin at the end of the workday when the weekend officially began.

"You know," Gisele said. "Fri-Yay?" She raised her hands up over her head, posing like a cheerleader.

Martha shook her head and returned to her work. Whatever was wrong with Gisele, she had gone past the point of her being able to help. She would not have been surprised if Gisele lost her job after all of this.

"Well, I'm gonna get to workin' it," Gisele said as she continued walking, throwing in dance moves to a song only she could hear.

The first stop Gisele made was the copy room. She was horny and figured Peter would be up for fucking her. She could see how that was a major shift in her thinking from a few days prior, but in her current state, it seemed like the perfect way to take care of her arousal. Her fingers could only do so much and she had not had a cock in her for almost a week. That seemed like far too long.

"Javier," Gisele whispered to herself, remembering the last time she had sex. A note of sadness seeped into her happy persona for a moment. She missed him. He was a good man.

And that was the truth. He had been a good man. Yes, he had his kinks. The bimbo kink was high among them it turned out. And Gisele was a bimbo now because of him and his device. Not that she understood what it was doing to her or why she seemed to be more of a bimbo now than she had been to start.

But the truth was, Gisele had never been so happy. She knew life without Javier would be different, but she was determined to make the most of it. He would want her to be happy. And she figured if she was happy as a bimbo, he would be all the more proud of her.

Gisele pushed the sadness away. She did not like to think about those sorts of things. She had been out looking for Peter and that was what she was going to continue to do.

"Oh, hey, Gisele," Peter said as she slipped into the copy room. She was about to drop to her knees again, but Peter had his arms full of papers and looked busy. "I'm sorry, but now's not a great time. I have deliveries to make. Maybe later?"

"Um, okay," Gisele said. She was disappointed for a moment, but then she remembered that he was not turning her down, just arranging for a later time. That could work for her. "Probably for the best. I need to go check in with my team."

"I like your dedication," Peter said. "You really care about the people who work for you."

Gisele stood up proudly, pushing her chest out. "Yeah, I guess I do."

"Good for you," Peter said. "That's a sign of a good

manager in my book. If only my dad believed in the same things."

Gisele found herself agreeing with Peter, although given that she had been about to seduce him, she would probably have agreed to anything he said. However, she felt good about the choice she had made the day before to suck his cock and the decision to get him to fuck her today. He was a man that needed rewarding.

The pair parted ways. Peter left to make his deliveries of various items that had been printed or copied. Gisele made her way to check in with her team. After the positive vibes she got from her in-person check-ins Thursday, she decided to make it a repeat event.

In reality, there were tasks that Gisele was actively avoiding. First and foremost was her monthly report and spreadsheet. She had not touched it and was hoping she could get away without completing it this month. Really, she hoped never to have to touch it again, but even she was not that naive.

However, unlike Thursday when Gisele simple spoke to the members of her team, this time she was a little more sensual about it. When someone looked tense, she took a moment to give them a shoulder massage. When they seemed panicky about getting all of their work done, she would see if another member of the team could take some of the load. She was doing her job, just in a very different manner than she used to.

And everyone, especially the men, but the women too, seemed to like Gisele's wardrobe choices. Placing here cleavage on full display had definitely been the right choice. Sometimes her massages would end with her letting them lean back and rest their head in her soft cleavage. Everyone seemed to enjoy that, although Gisele noticed a few of the male employees were tenting their pants after that.

As Giselle made her way back to her cubicle after checking in with everyone, she wondered if it would be appropriate for her to take care of her team in less conventional ways. Namely, she wondered if getting them off and providing other relaxation services would improve their productivity. Not that Gisele had a mind for that level of thinking. It was just a thought, but it did not remain for long, sitting untethered in her brain, as soon as her attention went elsewhere, it was forgotten.

When Gisele finally sat down at her desk for the first time that day, she found herself with a different kind of problem. While before her issues had been with how horny she could get, this time it had everything to do with her own forgetfulness.

Gisele forgot her computer password.

"Martha," Gisele called out while she continued to stare at her computer screen. The cursor in the password field blinked at her, judging her for her own stupidity and forgetfulness.

Martha came around the corner, always being there to help her coworker. "What's wrong?"

Gisele looked up at Martha with pleading eyes. "I forgot my password. Do you know it?"

Martha did not know whether to laugh or cry at her coworker's behavior. It was either funny, because Gisele always had a good memory before, or it was sad, because Gisele had never been this forgetful before.

"Why would I know your password?" Martha finally asked, taking a stern, but slightly playful, tone. "It's your password. Do you know my password?"

"Um," Gisele said, confused. There were two questions and she did not know which one she should answer. "I don't know. I… I don't know what to do."

It was a moment of honesty they both needed. Martha

had grown tired of Gisele's bimboish behavior, but she had been hoping she would finally open up. Maybe this was that moment.

"Here," Martha said, putting her arm around Gisele. "Let's go out to lunch together and you can explain everything. Then I can help you."

"You can?" Gisele asked, hopeful. She did not know if Martha meant she could help her with the computer password or with everything else. As much as Gisele liked being the company bimbo sexpot, she recognized that this was unusual behavior for her.

"Grab your purse," Martha said. "Let's go."

"Okie dokie," Gisele said, happy to have someone else leading the way. Managing a team was so hard. The people part was easy, but all the documentation and computer stuff seemed far too hard now. She was happy to have Martha as such a good friend to help her like this.

"Hey, Gisele," called Peter as she and Martha made their way to the exit. "I've got some free time now if you want to have that meeting."

Gisele looked back and nearly broke away from Martha. She had yet to cum since she arrived at work. She was horny and she was certain Peter would fuck her if she asked nicely. But as fun as that would be, Gisele needed Martha at the moment. And Peter would probably have some availability later in the day. She'd even consider going home with him if need be.

"Or maybe we can reschedule for the afternoon," Peter offered, seeing the pain in Gisele's eyes.

"I think that would be for the best," Martha said. "We're headed out for lunch."

"Cool, no problem."

Once Martha and Gisele were outside, Martha had to ask, "What was that about?"

"We have meetings," Gisele answered. She was not yet ready to admit she had given Peter a blowjob in the copy room and that she planned to ask him to fuck her. That was a bit too much at the moment. "We had to put off today's morning meeting."

"I see," Martha said, eyeing her coworker carefully. She was starting to better understand what Gisele had been up to, but she still had not figured out why.

Martha ordered wine for the both of them at lunch. She knew it might not be the professional thing to do, what with there still being at least four hours of work ahead of them, but she figured it would help Gisele loosen her tongue.

And loosen her tongue it did. Gisele told Martha everything. She talked about the device Javier had brought home from the lab, how she had been using it to let her keep working so she could keep paying her mortgage, and how she kept using it every night.

By this point, Gisele was not entirely sure why she kept using it each night. It had simply become habit. The reason why was forgotten much like she had forgotten her computer password.

"I can't believe it," Martha said after Gisele finished speaking. Admittedly, it had taken longer than normal for Gisele to explain everything, even with Martha holding her tongue and letting her coworker finally come clean. One of the effects of the device was as simplification of the vocabulary. With fewer words at her disposal, Gisele had a harder time explaining everything.

"It's true," Gisele said. "And it's kinda nice. I feel so good right now."

"But you have to let yourself process your feelings at some point," Martha said. "You can't keep running from your feelings forever."

Gisele shrugged. She did not see it that way anymore. She

could no longer comprehend the feelings she should have felt at Javier's passing. It was like a big positive bubble had filled her head, pushing out all of her negative thoughts. There simply was not room for them anymore.

"This device is intriguing," Martha admitted as their lunch wound down and they both began to sober up for the rest of their workday. "I kind of want to see it."

"Oh you should," Gisele said enthusiastically. "It's the best. It makes me feel super good."

"I can tell."

"Hey, you should come over tonight and try it," Gisele said as her face lit up with her idea. Good ideas were hard to come by for a bimbo like her. It usually required too much thinking.

"We'll see," Martha said, trying to be noncommittal. But the truth was, she wanted to try it. From the moment Gisele first described its effects, she wanted to try it. The stress of work was getting to her. It would be so much easier if she could shed that stress, even for a weekend.

"You said it's reversible, right?" Martha added.

"Yep. It's totally safe."

"Then I'll do it," Martha declared.

"Yay," Gisele said, clapping and bouncing in her seat. Her tits bounced, barely restrained by her blouse and jacket. Every male eye in the restaurant was watching her. Her bouncing and jiggling tits were like a beacon they could not turn away from.

"Can I follow you home after work?" Martha asked, planning their evening together. "I'll buy dinner."

"Who can say no to an offer like that?" Gisele said. "It's a date."

Gisele and Martha were both a little late returning from lunch. Luckily Mr. Marshall and the other supervisory staff were out at meetings offsite. No one seemed to mind as the two women returned, talking and laughing. It was an uncommon sound, but a welcome one, bringing a jovial quality the office environment sorely lacked.

Martha dove right back into her work. She still had the ability to switch gears. Gisele, however, did not. With her password still forgotten, she decided to go find Peter. Even if he did not know what to do about her password, she was certain he could finally scratch the itch that was her libido.

"You have a moment?" Gisele asked as she posed herself in the doorway to the copy room. She was still a little unsteady from the wine at lunch. Martha had ordered a bottle and Gisele drank most of it. She had less impulse control when she was in bimbo mode.

Peter looked up from the crossword he was working on. With upper management out of the building, his workload was less and he had a bit more free time.

"Hey there," Peter said. "I went looking for you a little while ago, but I couldn't find you. Looks like you had a good lunch."

"Sure did," Gisele agreed. It was so easy to agree with a man like Peter. "But now I'm here and I was hoping—"

"I've got the time," Peter said as he pushed his crossword puzzle aside.

"Good, 'cause I was hoping you could stick that nice cock of yours in my pussy," Gisele said after she closed the door behind her. "I'm super horny and I want to fuck."

Peter smiled. He was already undoing his belt as he rose to his feet. That was all the agreement they needed.

Gisele walked over to the copy machine, facing away from Peter. She started fiddling with her skirt. A moment later her thong panties appeared below the bottom of her skirt. She let them fall to her ankles before she stepped out of them.

"Won't be needing those right now," she said seductively as she kicked her panties across the room into the corner.

"No, I don't think you will," Peter said as he approached.

He stood behind Gisele and ran his hands along her shoulders and down her arms. She could sense his strength. He could do what he wanted with her, no matter what she did. He was stronger than her. He was faster than her. He was smarter than her.

Without saying a word, Peter guided Gisele into position. He bent her over the copy machine. She kept her legs straight, sticking out her ass into him. She could feel his hard cock through against her ass with only her skirt separating them.

Peter lifted Gisele's skirt in one smooth motion, bunching it up around her hips. That was all the access he would need.

"You're wet," Peter commented as he looked at her pussy.

"Always," Gisele breathed.

That had not always been true. But after so many bimbo layers added to her mind, her arousal had become a constant. She was always wet and ready.

"Good," Peter said calmly. "I like that."

Gisele smiled at the comment. And that smile only got wider when Peter finally did what he said he was going to do.

Gisele's pussy pulsed with pleasure as Peter slid into her. Her folds were wet and forgiving, but even then, she was forced to stretch around the girth of his cock.

"Oh yeah," Gisele moaned as her eyes rolled up into the back of her head under the onslaught of pleasure emanating from her pussy. It shot up her spine into her brain like small electric lightning bolts, carrying nothing but pleasure into her already bimbofied mind.

"You like this," Peter said.

"Like," Gisele responded, latching onto the word. It was an easy word, one she could remember. And she did like it.

She loved it. They had barely begun, but it was already the best sex that she could remember. Not that Gisele was a sex aficionado. But she knew what she liked and she liked this.

The copy machine rocked and shook as Peter pumped in and out of Gisele's hot pussy. Her tits were mashed against the machine, but she did not care. Nothing but the cock in her pussy mattered. Everything else was secondary to her primary objective to get her pussy fucked by Peter.

The moment Gisele felt Peter flood her channel with cum, she came too. She cried out, no longer able to hold her tongue, as her body convulsed with orgasmic energy. Her whole body got in on the action, her arms flailing about, her head lolling from side to side. Gisele's legs gave out on her, but that did not matter. She had the copy machine and Peter to support her.

"Wow," Gisele finally said as she started to come down from her orgasmic high. "That was super good."

For the first time that day, Gisele felt sexually satisfied. Even as she continued to lean over the copy machine, she could feel little aftershocks of her climax shoot through her, a reminder of the earth-shattering orgasm she had just experienced. Nothing compared.

"It was good," Peter agreed. "You're so tight. It's like you're perfect or something."

Gisele's mind was still not firing on all cylinders, but she smiled at the compliment. The idea of being perfect intrigued her. She could be the perfect bimbo, the perfect slut, the perfect woman. All it took was a little direction from a nice strong man like Peter.

It was more than 30 minutes after Gisele first arrived that she left the copy room. Her panties had gone forgotten in the corner, left behind fo the janitor to find. Not that Gisele paid any attention to her lack of panties. It felt natural to her now, to be so exposed and have the cool office air caress her most private areas. Panties were an option now, not a requirement.

What she did have, however, was Peter's phone number written on a piece of paper in her jacket pocket. She did not know if she would need his services over the weekend, but she felt comforted to know she had access to at least one cock in her time away from work.

When Gisele left the copy room, she had completely forgotten about her computer problems. She never did ask Peter about them. And rather than go back to her desk to be faced with the same problem again, Gisele found herself wandering around the office.

"You still doing okay?" Gisele asked one of her team members. She had given them a massage earlier in the day, but it did not hurt to check in on them for a second time.

"I'm great," he said, barely turning his head to greet his supervisor. "Thanks to your help, I'm almost done with this. It's the last thing I need to do before the weekend."

Gisele glanced at the clock, but she failed to read the time. Suddenly numbers, even ones like time, seemed a bit beyond her. She knew she should be worried about that, but it felt like too much of a hassle to worry about such a thing. It was nice not to have to worry about anything, or at least to not worry about anything. Life was much simpler and happier without worry being involved.

"Feel free to knock-off once you're done," Gisele said. "It's a beautiful Friday. Might as well enjoy as much of it as you can."

"Thanks, I'll do that," the employee responded.

It was not normal operating procedure to allow employees to leave early when they completed their work for the day. Company management wanted employees giving their all to the company during posted hours. Usually, an employee who left early or arrived late would be docked pay, assuming such a thing were caught.

However, with Gisele's tardiness not getting caught and with the senior leadership out of the building, Gisele opted for a morale based management system. She wanted to reward the people who worked for her for their hard work and their good work. If that meant someone left an hour early, that was fine by her.

By the time Gisele had finished making her rounds for a second time that day, she found herself standing at the entrance of Martha's cubicle.

"What say you and I cut out early," Gisele offered. "I've got nothing to do."

Martha grunted at first. She did not want to hear about Gisele's boredom. Martha had work to do. She had a lot of work to do. It was hard work managing her team.

Glancing at the clock, Martha sighed. She could sense she was out a crossroads with her current assignment. The next chunk of work would be a doozy and would take forever. It made little sense to start it now and then put it aside for the whole weekend. She would be spending just as much time Monday morning getting caught back up to speed on the project as she would now just to get started.

"All right," Martha finally said. "Let's go. I'm ready for the weekend to start."

Gisele smiled. This was much more fun that boring computer work.

The pair were once again walking out of the office, this time arm in arm. Gisele added an extra wiggle in her step, just for the fun of it, in case anyone got a good look at her ass on the way out the door.

As interested as Martha was in the device, she was in no real hurry to see it in action. The concept of it, while fascinating and a little arousing, was not something to be played with willy-nilly. Anything that affected the brain like it clearly did needed to be taken seriously.

However, once they reached Gisele's home, Martha could not find a good excuse not to at least look at it. Even after they called in a delivery order for pizza, the wait time was long enough for Gisele to show off her toy.

"It's super easy to use," Gisele explained as she attached the machine to her temples. "You just put these on and then turn it on. It can do more than bimbo mode, but I don't know how to change those settings. But you can make the wearer more of a bimbo or you can make them less of one. At least that's how it was explained to me."

"Can I see you use it?" Martha asked. Since Gisele was already hooked up, it made sense. "What happens?"

"Sure," Gisele answered. She felt perfectly comfortable going more bimbo, especially for the weekend. She could always change back later. "My mind is going to go blank while the machine works on my brain. But then I wake up feeling amazing."

Martha watched with great interest. She wanted to see it in action.

Gisele, meanwhile, set the device to add another layer of bimbo mode. She had previously been using it in the reverse mode, although she thought nothing of her need to make the switch. She did not think about those sorts of things anymore.

"Here we go," Gisele said as she activated the machine. It began to hum and a moment later everything for Gisele went dark and quiet.

The machine finished its work and then shut down. It was only a moment more before Gisele's eyes began to flutter and she woke up.

Gisele sat there for a moment. In front of her was Martha. That information did not make sense as she tried to put together what had just happened in her further bimbofied mind.

"Hi, Martha," Gisele finally said, punctuating it with a giggle.

Martha sat there dumbfounded. It had worked. Or at least it looked like it had worked. Gisele could have been faking it, but the difference between now and before she used the device saw an obvious dumbing effect. Gisele simply smiled and twirled her hair.

"How do you feel?" Martha asked, wanting confirmation that she felt as good as she looked.

Still wearing the attachments on her temples, Gisele figged her torso under her tits, lifting them in her arms before answering, "I feel super, super good. Like, I feel the best ever."

Martha could not be certain, but there was something in Gisele's voice that made her statement all the more believable. She sounded truly happy.

"I'm impressed," Martha said. "And you've been using it every night this week?"

"Yeppers," Gisele answered. "But I don't know how much more I can use it."

"Yeah, you seem pretty dumb right now. But as long as you're happy."

"That's right," Gisele said. "I'm happy."

Martha hesitated. There was a part of her that wanted to try the device on herself. She wanted to feel the happy bliss that seemed to embody Gisele to her very core. But mucking about with the brain was serious business. Could she really risk such a thing? What if it became permanent?

"Now it's your turn," Gisele said as she disentangled herself from the machine.

Panic struck Martha. "I don't know if I can..." she said, backing away.

"There's nothing to worry about," Gisele pressed. "It's fun and it feels really good. And we can totally undo it if you want."

Martha glanced at her watch. They had time before the pizza was ready. She could give it a try.

"Okay, hook me up."

Gisele enjoyed connecting Martha to the machine. She had never done this to someone else before. It had always been her on the receiving end of the mental changes. Now it would be her friend, for that was what they were becoming, friends.

As soon as Gisele was done, she handed Martha the device. It fit nicely in her lap.

"Switch it on when you're ready," Gisele prompted.

Martha looked down. It looked like a strange mix of computer parts in a black box. But the switch was clear. She just needed to flip it and it would activate.

"Here goes nothing," Martha said as she flipped the switch.

The machine began to hum and then her eyes closed. Gisele watched with rapt fascination as the device did its work.

It was not long before Martha began to stir. She opened her eyes to see Gisele grinning at her. Martha smiled back.

"How do you feel?" Gisele asked.

"I feel..." Martha said as she searched her mind for the right words. That had become harder, but not impossible given her single layer of bimbo programming. But what did she feel? She felt... good. That was the simplest way to say it and keeping things simple seemed like a good thing to do. "I feel good."

Gisele bounced in her seat and clapped. "Yay," she cheered. "And it gets better the more you use it."

"Um," Martha started to speak, wanting to voice her

desire not to go too far with a machine she had never used before, but it was hard to be negative with her mind in bimbo mode. "Maybe later," she eventually said. That allowed her time to think her situation through.

But the fact that it had worked made Martha feel all kinds of joy. She felt good. She felt happy. And did she feel horny? That was new, but not unwelcome.

Before the pair could think too much more about the machine or the bimbo life in general, the doorbell rang.

"That's the pizza," Martha said as she hopped up to answer the door. She was the one paying for it, after all. She had volunteered to do it since Gisele was hosting.

She did not hear Gisele mention that she was going to go change. They were both still wearing their work clothes and as much as Gisele wanted to hang out with Martha, she did not want to do so wearing her stuffy work outfit.

When Martha brought the pizza into the kitchen, Gisele was just finishing in the bedroom. She did not have time to change her makeup, but it was still in pretty good shape from her morning application. She did freshen her lipstick, because that was easy.

"Wow," Martha said when Gisele joined her in the kitchen.

Gisele giggled. "You like? I went shopping lsat night. Bought a bunch of new sexy clothes."

Sexy was right. Gisele had chosen an off the shoulder ruffled blouse that basically just covered her tits. It left her entire midriff bare as well as left a generous display of cleavage. And since they were not going anywhere, at least for the time being, she opted for a pair of short denim shorts. She wore a pair of wedge slides on her feet, keeping herself in high heels.

Martha could not tear her eyes away from Gisele. Yes, she was definitely a bimbo now. It was obvious the way she moved and dressed. Even her voice seemed to have a certain melodious quality that had not been there before.

"Wow," Martha said again. "You are so sexy."

"Thanks, babe," Gisele answered. "You know, if you get out of those work clothes, you can be pretty sexy too."

"Um," Martha said. "I'm not sure I'm ready for that yet. Let's eat first."

The pizza was good and the two women enjoyed their evening together. They laughed. They giggled, they drank some more wine, and Martha used the device twice more to get an even bigger bimbo effect.

As the evening turned into night, Gisele offered Martha her spare bedroom. Neither of them wanted to go out driving this late, not that either of them were capable at that moment. Wine and mind-altering machines do not necessarily mix.

Martha was only too happy to accept such a kind offer. And as a reward for Gisele, Martha used the machine one last time before she went to sleep so that her dreams could be filled with bimbo goodness.

Gisele woke up Saturday morning naked and with her hand in her pussy. That had become the norm. Not that Gisele was complaining. If her hand needed to be somewhere, it might as well be in her pussy. It felt good and she was horny. It was a win-win as far as she could figure.

It was only when Martha found herself mincing into the kitchen wearing her wedge slides, which basically served as her house slippers now, and a thin robe that she had failed to tie shut, that she saw the machine on the kitchen table and the previous night's events returned to her.

"That was fun," Gisele said to herself. But she was aware that she would need more than just a partner in crime when it came to acting like a bimbo. She was going to need some more cock and sooner rather than later.

"Morning, sleep head," Gisele said as she peaked into the spare bedroom. She had yet to close her robe, but she was past the point of caring about that. She was a sexy young woman. Why should she hide herself, especially at home around friends?

And it was not like Martha was in a decent position

herself. The newly minted bimbo was sleeping much like Gisele had, naked and with her hands between her legs.

"Hmm," Martha said as she rolled over and stretched. Gisele could tell she had a good night. It was so much easier to sleep as a bimbo. With no worries to bother her, she earned a solid night's sleep.

"Come on, Martha," Gisele said. "It's time to get up."

Martha opened her eyes to see her friend standing in the doorway. She felt no shame in her nudity, nor in Gisele's revealing robe. Martha smiled.

"Good morning," Martha said before she blissfully yawned.

"You sleep good?"

"Really good," Martha answered. "But I'm horny." That last bit came out as a whine.

"Then cum, silly," Gisele said. "Use your fingers."

"Oh, yeah," Martha said, having forgotten about the possible solutions to her high arousal.

"But don't take too long," Gisele continued. "We need to go shopping for you. Can't have a sexy bimbo like you wearing work clothes all weekend."

"Yeah," Martha moaned in agreement. But she was already far too gone to really comprehend what Gisele had said. Her focus was on her fingers penetrating her pussy. That was what mattered.

With Martha up and close to cumming, Gisele decided it was time for her to get ready. She really did intend on taking Martha shopping. She needed bimbo clothes to match her bimbo brain.

Of course, given Gisele's natural proclivities, no morning was complete without an orgasm or two. Or in Gisele's case, it was three. Once she started, she just found it so hard to stop. Anything and everything could be a source of arousal.

The hot spray from the shower or even just a stray thought could get her juices flowing.

It took three hours for the two bimbos to be dressed and ready to go out.

"Uh, uh, uh," Gisele said when Martha made her move toward the door.

"What?" Martha asked, not understanding what her host wanted.

"Time for another bimbo layer," Gisele said, holding out the device.

Martha considered her situation for a moment. That did sound fun. But how many times had she used it and how many times had Gisele. Martha started to count on her fingers. It was one of the few ways she could still count. Without a visual reference, she had a hard time remembering what she had counted already.

It took several minutes, but Martha eventually realized she had used the machine four times already. And if Gisele's story had been accurate, which was not guaranteed, it meant she had used it six times. Or was it seven? She could not be sure. It was so easy to lose track once a second hand's worth of fingers was needed.

Either way, Martha realized she still had a ways to go before she caught up to Gisele. And since Gisele seemed like a fully functioning adult, even if she was a bimbo, it would not hurt to use the machine again. It would certainly make shopping a lot more fun.

By the time the pair reached the mall, it was already mid-afternoon. And by then, Martha had actually used the machine two more times. She was feeling very bimboey indeed with a big smile on her face, a wet pussy, and an attention span of a gnat. But she had fun, which was all that mattered.

Gisele and Martha visited many of the same stores Gisele

had visited Thursday night, but this time it was all about Martha getting the bimbo wardrobe she needed. And Martha was certainly not someone who was going to argue. She practically skipped from store to store, excited at all the different tops, skirts and dresses she had bought.

But it was her new high heels collection that Martha was most proud of. She had never cared for them before, but now that she was a bimbo, she did not want to wear anything else on her feet. Even her trainers for the gym had a heel on them.

Of course, Gisele could not keep herself from making some purchases as well. She was a bimbo and as such, she had absolutely no impulse control. But she kept her personal shopping to a minimum, focusing on a few select items, like bikinis for when the summer rolled around, and makeup, since her normal collection was inadequate at best.

At the end of the trip, Gisele's car was filled to the brim with purchases and both women looked like they were ready to win a slut contest, had there been one. It took them many trips to bring all of Martha's new purchases into the house. The parade attracted quite a bit of attention in the neighborhood, with neighbors watching the two women go back and forth between the car and the front door, both from windows and from the sidewalk as several neighbors decided it was the perfect time to take their dogs for walks, regardless of the actual need.

For their part, both Gisele and Martha enjoyed the attention. They added an extra sway to their strides. In Gisele's case, she also added some shoulder action to make sure her tits bounced in her low-cut top. Martha was unable to up her game in the chest department, since she was not as well endowed as her bimbo friend.

Despite no formal agreement, Martha's new clothes went into the closet of Gisele's spare bedroom. Clothes needed hanging up, at the very least, but there was an unspoken understanding that Martha might end up moving into the spare room. It seemed like a natural extension of their friendship, as long as they were still bimbos.

Once everything was neat and tidy in the closet, having emptied it of documents and other storage items from Gisele's less interesting, pre-bimbo life, it was time to play with the device again.

"Are you sure I should?" Martha asked as the pair sat at the kitchen table with the device between them. Gisele had already hooked Martha up to the machine. Not that Martha was seriously questioning Gisele's intentions. She always enjoyed coming out of her blank state and finding herself happier and hornier. When those feelings did not subside, it was difficult to say no. It was like a drug where the high never wore off.

"It'll be fun," Gisele said. "You know you want to."

Martha looked back down at the device. She did want to. That was part of the problem. Or at least that was what the more lucid parts of her brain were telling her. She just wanted to feel more of the bimbo bliss. Then again, she told herself it could all be reversed before work on Monday. She could let loose and have a fun bimbo-filled weekend.

Before Gisele could say more and before Martha could talk herself out of it, Martha activated the machine and let it add another bimbo layer to her mind. Her brain shut down faster than ever as it allowed the device to access her mind. She was left completely unaware as Gisele pulled her brief skirt up around her waist to give herself easy access to her pussy so she could masturbate to the further bimbofication of her friend.

When Martha opened her eyes, she giggled. "I'm horny," she announced, without a filter between her thoughts and her mouth. Everything she thought, she said.

"Good," Gisele said. "Now do it again."

Martha sat there for a moment, processing Gisele's words. Her mind worked so much more slowly than before. It left long gaps in their conversations as they worked to understand what each other was saying. Martha's mind in particular, struggled. Her use of the device came much more frequently, having equaled Gisele's level of bimbofication in the span of 24 hours. Gisele reached the same point after six days.

Martha was past the point of disagreeing. She reached out her hand and activated the machine again. Her blackout came even sooner as she closed her eyes and simply sat there. Martha was completely unaware of anything going on around her as the device did its work. She could see nothing, she could hear nothing, she could taste and smell nothing, and she could not feel anything. Her mind, her body, were complete blanks.

When Martha opened her eyes again, her eyes registered what she saw, but her mind could not seem to turn those images into thoughts. It was as if there was a short circuit in her mental processing, preventing her from accessing the images created by her eyes.

This was true for all of Martha's senses. She was completely cut off from the world outside her body. Her brain was capable of creating thoughts, but it seemed uninterested in doing so.

"Wakey wakey," Gisele finally said as she unhooked the device from Martha's temples and put the machine away. "It's time to get ready for the club."

As Martha sat there, unhearing of her friend's words, she had one overpowering emotion. It was happiness. Nothing else in that moment seemed to matter. It was a feeling that had grown inside of herself. It glowed brightly, warming her from the inside, giving her the only sensations she could experience in that opening moment.

Martha smiled aimlessly, her expression one of extreme happiness and bliss. There was nothing that could get her down. She had an impenetrable shield, a candy coating that would not melt away, keeping her perpetually positive.

"Club?" Martha finally asked, a note of confusion on her face.

Gisele thought Martha looked particularly cute when she was confused. Her eyebrows rose in surprise and she placed a finger at the side of her mouth, looking off into nothing as her brain tried to process the sounds she heard and the images she could now see.

"It'll be fun," Gisele prodded. "Let's get dressed up nice and sexy and go find some guys to fuck."

"I like to fuck," Martha said almost automatically, as if it was a pre-recorded response.

"Of course you do," Gisele said. "You're a bimbo now. Bimbos like to fuck."

"Yeah," Martha agreed. "I'm a bimbo. I like to fuck."

Both women broke out in a fit of giggles. Even Gisele thought they might have used the device too much on Martha. She had become a complete idiot. But who cared about intelligence when sex was on the brain. And as bimbos, sex was definitely on both of their minds.

Gisele guided Martha to what was basically her new bedroom to allow her to get ready. Gisele wondered if Martha was even too dumb now to dress herself for the club, but Gisele had her own outfit to change into and her makeup to do. She wanted to look sexy, slutty, and easy. That took some work.

Once alone, Martha finally started to snap out of her mental fog. She was still not all there, but her mind was once again operating, albeit on a single cylinder that was a single distraction away from failing again.

Martha opted for a sparkly bra top and a matching sparkling skirt, both in a pinkish purple color that seemed to switch between the two depending on what angle she was viewed from. The pink high heels completed the outfit.

After that, Martha spent her time trying to get her hair and makeup to look just right. For her hair, she wore it down, letting it fall to her shoulder blades in back and down to the top slope of her tits in front. She wished she had longer hair, as well as bigger tits, but for tonight, she would work with what she had. There were ways to get longer hair and bigger tits, but she had more pressing matters to attend to first.

Gisele, meanwhile, needed a little more time to decide on what to wear. She slowly narrowed her choices down to three dresses. The first was practically see-through, requiring her to wear panties and pasties over her nipples. The second was a purple halter dress with a neckline that fell to below her belly-button and barely covered her ass, leaving the entirety of her back bare. The third dress was yellow and featured random cutouts and rips in strategic places to make it clear she was not wearing underwear underneath, while keeping her modesty intact.

After much debating, Gisele finally chose the purple dress. It just seemed to fit the evening so much better. And it certainly gave any man she met easier access to her body. The less fabric that got in the way, the better. And luckily, Gisele had a matching pair of purple heels with a spiked heel and a platform that added two inches under her toes.

"Perfect," Gisele told her reflection once she finished styling her hair and makeup. She looked nothing like the respectable woman she had been the week before. Now she was a complete bimbo. Her single programming layer from her first experience with the device would never have allowed her to dress like such a slut for a night on the town.

But this version of Gisele, the one that had used the device every night for six nights in a row, had no qualms with her appearance. She took a moment to shift her tits in the dress, making them more prominent and more visually appealing. That was important to her now. She wore tight and sexy dresses to give men something to look at. It was all the better if they wanted to fuck her. If they were hot enough, she would want to fuck them too.

Both bimbos came out of their rooms at about the same time. Martha squealed when she saw Gisele. The pair embraced, with Gisele planting a sensuous kiss on Martha's lips. Martha, loving the physicality of Gisele's lips on hers, returned it with vigor.

"We better get going," Gisele said when she finally broke the kiss. "We've got cock to find."

And with that, the pair left Gisele's house, hailing a ride to take them downtown to some of the cities trendiest clubs. Neither of them had been clubbing before, at least not at this level, but that did not matter. No one would have guessed at their inexperience in such matters when they showed up at the front door of the Lucky Seven and were waved in by the bouncer, passing a long line of people looking to get in. It paid to dress like a slut for just that reason.

As Gisele and Martha danced it up at the Lucky Seven, looking for action, there was a different kind of action taking place back at Gisele's house. The door had been left unlocked. Gisele left her keys at home, since she did not have a good place to keep them. Her little clutch purse could only hold so much.

There was no breaking, just entering. It had taken just a few hours for Javier's former employer to determine that he was the source of the theft. That was Monday morning. It had taken them five days to discover where he had hidden the stolen device.

The car sitting outside Gisele's house went unnoticed when the two women left for the Lucky Seven. As soon as they were out of sight, the occupant of the car, a tall muscular man wearing a black suit, including sunglasses after dark, got out and walked up the front path.

He tried the front door. It was always the first thing he checked on assignments like this. Sometimes the door was left unlocked. This was one of those times, making it easy for him to slip inside undetected.

The man knew nothing of what the device he was looking for did. He had been briefed on its components and what it looked like, but nothing else. Such matters as purpose were on a need to know basis and the man did not need to know.

While the two bimbos were dancing their asses off to their hearts content, the man was in Gisele's home, searching room to room. It turned out to be even easier than he had imagined. The two women had left the device out not he kitchen table.

It only took a brief inspection to make sure all the missing pieces were present. After that, he scooped up the device and walked back out to his car. Easiest money he had ever made on a nighttime caper such as this.

However, before driving away, the man made a mental note of the house number one last time. He had seen the two women leaving. They were hot and slutty and definitely his type. He liked them dumb, which the two giggling bimbos seemed fully embrace. He bet they would be fun to fuck as a threesome.

Back at the Lucky Seven, it did not take long before the two new bimbos made quite a name for themselves. They started by landing two guys, best friends out for a night on the town, much like they were. However, rather than arrange to leave the club, they found their way into a room in the back, a space the club sometimes used for private events on quiet nights. Tonight, the room was empty.

Gisele and Martha acted almost in tandem as they dropped to their knees. Moments later, they each had a mouth full of cock. They sucked away while the two men high-fived each other at scoring so early in their night.

The men came at roughly the same time, leaving Gisele and Martha to quickly swallow their cum. It was only the second blow job for both women, but the two men never would have guessed. They sucked cock like seasoned bimbos, as if the device had more than made them dumb and horny sluts, but implanted a level of sexual experience to go with it. Not that anyone was complaining. Both women found they loved to suck cock and the two men certainly enjoyed it from their perspectives. It was a win-win.

The secret room proved to be a fantastic place to keep going with their sexy fun that night at the club. Gisele and Martha took turns with the men they hooked up with, dragon them to the back of the building and either sucking cock or having what was left of their brains fucked out of them.

Martha, who had used the device one extra time compared to Gisele, seemed especially insatiable. It was as if she had previously lived a monastic life and was now making up for lost time. While Gisele took her time before she got to sex, Martha practically jumped guys on the dance floor. It was only on their insistence that they go someplace more private. And it was not uncommon for Martha to take more than one man back with her when it was her turn. Whether they fucked her in the mouth, pussy, or ass did not seem to matter much to Martha. She just wanted as much cock inside of her as possible and as often as possible. Getting tag-teamed or shared made it all the better.

When Gisele and Martha finally stumbled home, manless, but well and truly fucked, they were too out of it to notice the missing piece of equipment from the kitchen table. Their drunkenness did not help matters either. What was a bimbo to do when she was offered a free drink by an attractive man? She drank it, of course.

The pair collapsed into their respective beds, barely having the wherewithal to clean their makeup off their faces and take off their clothes from the night. Martha was asleep almost before her head hit the pillow. For Gisele, her sleep came a moment later, only after thinking how great a time she had and how lucky she was to be a bimbo.

MONDAY

By the time Monday morning rolled around, Gisele and Martha were struggling to get ready for work. The hardest part was choosing something appropriate to wear.

In Martha's case, she was basically helpless. She could have worn the same outfit from Friday. It was still sitting there crumpled up in the corner of her new bedroom, but Martha had no interest in wearing that again. It lacked every bimbo quality she now held dear.

And her new purchases were not helping matters. Martha had gone shopping with the club in mind, not work. And as hot as it would be to show up at the office looking like she was ready to go out on the town, deep down she realized that would only lead to getting fired. As much as her job no longer appealed to her, she needed the money, at least to pay off the credit cards she had maxed out on her Saturday afternoon shopping trip.

The fact Martha had yet to return home did not bother her. Then again, nothing significant bothered Martha anymore. It was only what most people considered insignificant that bothered her now. Namely, that was looking pretty and sexy.

For Gisele, she was more prepared. She had the available clothing to choose from. But for her, what slowed her down, as it did most mornings, was her own libido. That had only seemed to strengthen over the weekend. She had lost count of the number of times she came, not that it mattered. The more orgasms the better as far as she was concerned.

First there had been the Sunday morning call to Peter. He was happy to come over and fuck both Gisele and Martha. He needed time to recover, but she made sure both of them were well fucked.

Then there was another man that showed up after Peter left. Gisele could not remember him, but he seemed familiar with her. And he was hot, being tall and muscular. Martha had been the one to answer the door and she was the one who led him inside.

Although it had been his idea to fuck them both over the kitchen table. First he fucked Martha with her screaming through multiple orgasms. Then he did the same to Gisele. And finally, he fucked them both, trading off between the two as they lay bent over the table, side-by-side. He came on their bare backs, a compromise since he could not cum in both their pussies.

Gisele never did get the man's name. He promised to be back, which both bimbos were only too glad to encourage. Martha was past the point of caring about names. As long as there was a cock, she was happy. The name that went with it was superfluous to her bimbofied brain.

But no matter how many times Gisele came over the weekend, she was still left aroused beyond the point of being able to fully function Monday morning. It was only after she came three times, one with the help of Martha's surprisingly talented tongue, that she could even begin to think about going into work.

When the pair finally arrived, it was clear that something was different from the moment they stepped through the front doors. Eyes peeked up above the cubicle walls as they two bimbos clicked and clacked their way through the office.

Gisele looked moderately professional, ignoring the fact her tits were ready to pop out of her blouse and her skirt was short enough that she could not bend over without flashing everyone behind her, showing them she wore no panties.

Martha finally found something that might be considered office appropriate. She wore a pink strapless bandage body con dress. Normally it would have been too short to cover both her tits and her ass in a professional manner. But she had paired it with a tied-off white blouse, allowing the dress to sit lower on her body, as well as make it obvious she was not wearing a bra. With breasts of her small size, she did not feel the need to wear a bra anymore.

But it was not just the fact the two women walked in late and turned heads. The senior management team had returned and they were not happy.

Gisele dropped Martha off at the copy room. Peter would be able to look after her until Gisele was ready to resume bimbo sitting duties. Martha, having completely embraced her many layers of bimbo programming, was left unable to fully function in society. She needed constant supervision or she would get herself into trouble. Gisele was usually able to fill that role, but someone else would need to step in some-times. Peter was a perfect choice in that regards.

After leaving Martha to suck Peter's cock, Gisele made her way to Mr. Marshall's office. It seemed fitting that Mr. Marshall's son, Peter, was helping Gisele with her plan. Now to make the big boss see things her way.

"What the hell has gotten into you?" Mr. Marshall started

screaming as soon as Gisele stepped into his office. The door was not even shut before he laid into her.

Gisele simply stood there in front of his desk as he pushed himself to his feet to yell all the louder. He was angry to say the least, and to a certain degree, Gisele could see why. From his view, her behavior was unacceptable. It was going to be her job to make him see otherwise.

Using her bimbo positivity, Gisele was able to withstand the onslaught of Mr. Marshall's anger. She simply stood there, pushing her chest out, smiling, and letting her fractured memories from the weekend play out in her mind.

It took at least 20 minutes, but Mr. Marshall's sails finally deflated. Hoarse, he took a deep breath and sagged against his desk, supporting himself with both arms, his head drooping.

"What do you have to say to that?" Mr. Marshall asked.

Gisele, who had heard nothing of what he had said in his outburst, had finally started to pay attention again.

"You're looking at this all wrong, Mr. Marshall," Gisele said with a sweet smile. "Have you looked at last week's efficiency numbers for my team?"

Mr. Marshall grumbled for a moment before he opened the file on his desk. He had not actually read them yet. It was usually the first thing he did every Monday morning, but hearing the stories of Gisele's antics from Friday, along with the possible corruption of Martha, his focus had been elsewhere.

"They're up?" Mr. Marshall said, surprised.

"I did something different last week," Gisele said. "I encouraged my team. I took care of them. Rather than ordering them around, I listened and made sure they had what they needed to be successful. And I only did that for two days. We those numbers go up from two days of warmer and more supportive managing."

"But the way you're dressed, showing up late, not being at your desk," Mr. Marshall listed. "That's all bad."

"Mr. Marshall," Gisele said as she began a slow walk around the desk, making sure to emphasize the sway of her hips. "I don't think you understand what a woman like me can do for morale. No one likes to work here. The pay is low, the benefits worse. But we feel stuck. I help make my team actually want to work here and because of that, they work better and harder. Let me show you."

Gisele gracefully dropped to her knees, something she had become well-practiced in over the past week. Mr. Marshall turned to face his employee, but that only served to give her the access she needed.

"You're too tense, Mr. Marshall," Gisele said with lust lidded eyes. "Let me help you with that. Maybe I can add a smile to your face too."

Gisele used all her skills as she went down on her boss. She did not do this to save her job. She was certain she would land on her feet somewhere. But she needed to show senior managers, like Mr. Marshall, that they needed to make changes. They needed to remember that sometimes spending money was required to make money. And spending money on the employees and their morale was money well spent to improve the bottom line.

After Mr. Marshall came in Gisele's mouth, he collapsed into his chair, but a broad smile had formed on his face.

"That was…" he started to say, but lost track of what words he wanted to use. "That was amazing. I always wanted to know what that felt like."

"You have a nice, big, and tasty cock, Mr. Marshall," Gisele said as she sat back on her heels. "I have a feeling after that tension relief you're feeling better and happier."

"Yes," Mr. Marshall agreed. "Definitely yes."

"So you can see that maybe giving your employees a morale boost might be a good idea?"

Mr. Marshall got a twinkle in his eye. "Yes, I think something like that can be arranged. I will need to clear it with the management team, but I think we need a chief morale officer. But I'm concerned. We can't pay you to suck off every guy on staff when they're unhappy. That's not only illegal, it's not possible."

Gisele smiled as she carefully rose to her feet. She circled around Mr. Marshall as he continued to sit in his chair. She came up behind him and let his head rest in her cleavage as she began to slowly massage his shoulders.

"It's not all about sex," Gisele said. "Sometimes a little massage or relaxation or soothing and encouraging words are all that's needed. You can understand that, can't you, Mr. Marshall?"

Gisele looked down to see Mr. Marshall's cock making a valiant effort to recover from her earlier ministrations. She smiled, knowing she had him.

"Oh, yes," Mr. Marshall groaned. "But the rest of the management team will need convincing."

"I think that can be arranged, Mr. Marshall. But you know, it is a really big job. I'm just a dumb bimbo now. I can't even remember my computer password anymore. Did you know that? So if I'm going to be chief morale officer, or whatever, I'm going to need two things. I'm going to need someone to handle the paperwork and scheduling. I think the copy room guy would be great for that. I'm also going to need an assistant. Martha's a bimbo now too and she would be great at raising the spirits of your employees."

"Yes," Mr. Marshall said. "Yes, whatever you want. I'll clear it with management. And that's my son by the way. But you're right. The copy room is too small a job for him. He needs some real responsibility. And that promotion might get him to move out of the basement. He can't afford rent on the copy room salary."

"Oh, thank you, Mr. Marshall," Gisele said enthusiastically. "You make me so happy to hear that. And don't you be a stranger, you hear? I want to make sure your morale is high too."

Gisele came back around the chair to face Mr. Marshall straight on. She bent down, bending at the waist like a good bimbo should, and kissed the head of his cock before she put him away.

As Gisele slipped out of her boss' office, she heard him pick up the phone at bark at his secretary. She still had her work cut out for her, but she was certain to change things in the office for the better. With her and Martha handling morale duties, there were going to be a lot more smiles in the office.

However, after Gisele sucked Mr. Marshall's cock, she found herself horny. She needed a good fucking and she knew just who to visit.

When Gisele reached the copy room, she found Martha sitting up on the copy machine, but Peter was nowhere to be seen.

"Peter left for work stuff," Martha said. Even though she was bored, she still had a smile on her face.

"I've got some good news," Gisele announced. "First, we've got new jobs. Peter will too. We're part of the new morale team. Mr. Marshall's still working out the details. We might need to convince some of the other bosses. But this whole change means I'm going to be your boss now."

"Yay," Martha cheered as she bounced off the copy machine, jumping around and clapping.

"I know you can fuck and suck like a good bimbo," Gisele continued. "But I want to know if you can lick pussy like one too."

Without even thinking, Martha dropped to her knees in front of Gisele. She had never eaten pussy before, but as far as she could tell she had always wanted to. And without even thinking, she started, sending Gisele to never before felt heights. Everything was looking up for the two new office bimbos.

Life at the office had changed for everyone. For the first time in recent memory, employees actually wanted to come into work. They felt supported and willing to give their all.

That turnaround was all because of Gisele and her morale management team. Peter managed the logistics, making sure there was a schedule. He reached out to people, checking in on them, seeing what kind of help they might need.

Gisele had become man expert at motivating people. She was not the office sexpot that she thought she might become. She was the classy morale officer. She listened to people's thoughts. She massaged their shoulders when they were tense. She let people rest their heads on her soft breasts if they needed to relax.

It was Martha who became the office sexpot. Of course, under Gisele's guidance she even more looked the part compared to that first weekend. The surgeries had been important, getting Martha's body up to fucktoy status. Her tits were large and round, each as big as her head.

Her ass had been enhanced as well. Martha simply did not have the discipline to build it herself in the gym. Gisele managed that for herself, but Martha could not always control her assistant.

And since Martha was going all in on the fucktoy body, she had everything else done to enhance her sexiness too. Lip fillers, a nose job, she even had her floating ribs removed to give her a smaller waist. Anything and everything to make her a better office bimbo.

She was a big hit with everyone in the office. Martha had combined science and art to perfect office sex for the benefit of morale.

It did help that Martha officially moved in with Gisele. She could not have afforded her old place anymore after her bimbofication. Martha spent almost all of her free cash on clothes. Gisele was not much better, but they both had Peter to handle the financial side of their lives. At least Gisele was able to compensate for some of her new spending habits with her higher salary. But again, Peter still managed it. She was too much of a bimbo to remember to have money for the mortgage payment every month.

But the truth of the matter was everyone was happy with the results. Neither Gisele nor Martha ever worried about the machine that had turned them into bimbos. They no longer cared about it. They did not even realize it had gone missing.

The only sign that something had happened was the man who would show up to fuck them both on the weekends. Not that either of them minded. They still did not know his name, but they appreciated all he did for them.

As for the events that led to this new reality, they remained largely forgotten by Gisele, much like she forgot her computer password. Her life had new meaning now. She had no idea it all came about because of a tragic event and a computer error. Not that she, nor anyone else, was complaining. Becoming a bimbo was the best thing that had ever happened to her and Martha and they loved every moment of it.

ABOUT THE AUTHOR

Sadie Thatcher is a longtime author of erotic fiction, especially related to transformations and bimbofication. She likes to say "I have thrown off the shackles of my conservative upbringing and now write erotic stories."

She maintains several blogs devoted to her writings, including a behind the scenes look at her writing process, and bimbos in general, as well as highlights works by other authors. They can be found at:

https://authorsadiethatcher.tumblr.com
https://buildingbettergiggles.tumblr.com

Subliminal Society

Inheritance

The Curse of Playing Bimbo Tag

The Curse of Playing Bimbo Tag: Jenna or Jenni

The Bimbo Professor: The Curse of Playing Bimbo Tag Book 3

Anything for the Job

Anything for the Job 2

Anything for His Job

Bimbo Halloween

Bimbo Christmas

Dorm Room Bimbo

Carissa's Magic Pen

Spirit Walk

Muscle Memory

The Case of the Bimbo Wife

Changes

New Year New You

The Bimbo Dream

The Wedding Gift

The Cure

Backfire

Body Swap Rings: Happy Anniversary

Body Swap Rings 2: Wedding Night

The Bimbo Experience

The Bimbo Experience 2

The Bimbo Experience 3some

The 4th Bimbo Experience

Bimbo Genes

Bimbo Genes II: The Virus

The Bimbo Genes III: The Epidemic

www.ingramcontent.com/pod-product-compliance
Lightning Source LLC
Chambersburg PA
CBHW020459160726
47991CB00007B/2731